The Emerald Princess Finds a Fairy

THE JEWEL KINGDOM

The Emerald Princess Finds a Fairy

JAHNNA N. MALCOLM

Illustrations by Neal McPheeters

SCHOLASTIC INC.
NEW YORK   TORONTO   LONDON   AUCKLAND   SYDNEY

ISBN 0-590-11738-6

12 11 10 9 8 7 6 5 4 3 2   8 9/9 0 1 2 3/0

Printed in the U.S.A.   40
First Scholastic printing, April 1998

For Katie and Bill,
and their little princesses,
Annie and Caroline

CONTENTS

The Emerald Princess Finds a Fairy

THE JEWEL KINGDOM

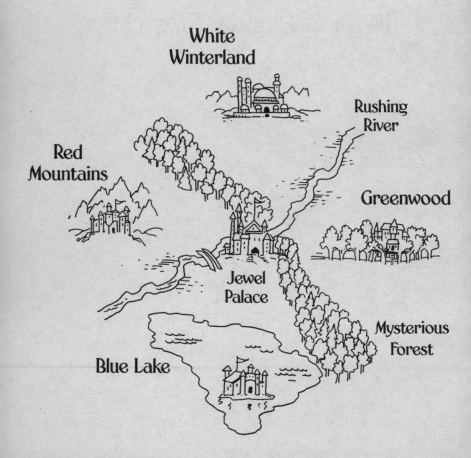

White
Winterland

Rushing
River

Red
Mountains

Greenwood

Jewel
Palace

Mysterious
Forest

Blue Lake

The Forest of Flowers

"I'm bored," Princess Emily complained to her friend Arden. "Nothing exciting ever happens in the Greenwood."

"How can you say that?" the beautiful white Unicorn replied. "Last week the Shinnybins raced the Nutgrubs. They ran the entire length of the Greenwood, from the Rushing River to the Mysterious Forest."

The Emerald Princess ran one hand through her thick red hair. "That was fun to watch. But it wasn't very exciting. We knew the Shinnybins would win."

Shinnybins were long-armed creatures that lived in the treetops. Because they were so fast, Princess Emily often used them to carry messages to her friends on the other side of the Greenwood.

"I wish something thrilling would happen," Emily said as she walked through the Forest of Flowers. In the Forest of Flowers, every flower was very large and always in bloom.

"You mean you want something *bad* to happen?" the Unicorn asked, weaving her way between the tall stalks of lavender.

"Not exactly bad," Emily said. "But maybe just a little bit dangerous." Her green eyes flashed as she added, "I'd like to have a real adventure."

"Would you like to play hide-and-seek in these flowers?" Arden tossed her long white mane. "That can be an adventure. You never know what is hiding under these huge blooms."

The Emerald Princess sighed. "Hide-and-seek wasn't what I had in mind."

"Come on, Princess," Arden coaxed, nudging Emily's elbow with her velvety nose. "It could be very fun."

Emily knew she was being silly to wish for something dangerous to happen in the Greenwood. After all, it was her land. And she was supposed to take care of it.

When she and her three sisters were crowned the Jewel Princesses, their parents, Queen Jemma and King Regal, gave each princess her own land to rule.

Emily was given the Greenwood, a forest of giant cedars and elms. The Emerald Palace was a wonderful tree house with ropes and ladders. It had lots of windows with brightly painted shutters.

Emily's oldest sister, Princess Demetra, was crowned the Diamond Princess. She ruled the White Winterland, a magical place of snow and ice.

Roxanne, the Ruby Princess, lived in the Ruby Palace high in the rocky Red Mountains.

Sabrina, the Sapphire Princess, ruled from her blue-and-white palace in the middle of Blue Lake.

The Jewel Kingdom was a happy place to live. And Emily wanted it to stay that way.

"All right, Arden," the princess said.

"I'll hide. Close your eyes and count to twenty-five."

The Unicorn closed her big brown eyes and began to count. "One, two, three . . ."

Emily raced through the Forest of Flowers. She spied a circle of buttercups and bellflowers. It was the perfect place to hide.

She ducked under the flower petals and dropped to her knees.

"Ouch!" a tiny voice cried. "That hurts. Please, get off me!"

Emily sprang to her feet. "Who said that?"

"Me!" the voice answered.

"Where are you?" Emily asked, spinning in a circle.

"Down here," the voice replied. "I'm standing on this buttercup."

Emily bent down and stared at the big

yellow flower. A little girl, no more than six inches tall, was standing on one of its petals.

The little girl had blonde curly hair, delicate pointed ears, and beautiful lavender wings with flecks of gold. She wore a dress made of red flower petals.

"You're a Fairy!" Emily cried.

The Fairy covered her ears and hid behind one of the petals.

"I didn't mean to frighten you," Emily said in a softer voice. She knelt between the buttercups to get a better look at the tiny Fairy.

She seemed to be about Emily's age. She had a dusting of freckles across her nose, just like Emily. But this Fairy had lavender eyes. Emily's were bright emerald green.

"I haven't seen very many Fairies in the

Greenwood," Emily explained. "I know Hazelnut. She is a friend of Staghorn, our palace gardener. And Ivy. But I've never seen you before."

"That's because I don't live here," the little Fairy replied, peeking her head out from behind the petal.

"Where do you live?" Emily asked.

The little Fairy carefully straightened her lavender wingtip. "I can't tell you that."

"I didn't mean to hurt your wing," Emily said. "I hope it's not broken."

"I've heard stories about Giants crushing Fairies," the little Fairy said. "But I never thought it would happen to me."

Emily blinked in surprise. "I'm not a Giant."

"You look like a Giant," the Fairy said, staying behind the flower. "You have big hands and big feet. And big scary teeth."

"I do not!" Emily shouted.

This frightened the little Fairy. She flew away from Emily and hid inside a blue bellflower.

"Oh, dear," Princess Emily murmured. "Now I've done it."

The princess crossed to the bellflower and whispered, "I promise I won't shout again. Please come out."

"No," a tiny voice replied. "You're too big. And too scary."

"What if I were small?" Princess Emily asked. "Would you come out then?"

After a long pause, the little voice answered, "Maybe."

Emily reached for her magic pan flute. The great wizard Gallivant had given it to her when she was crowned a Jewel

Princess. The magic flute had the power to make her very large or very small. All she had to do was blow the right note.

The princess took a deep breath and blew the very highest note.

Princess Arabell

———◆———

The Emerald Princess was now six inches tall. She was exactly the same height as the little blonde Fairy.

Emily flopped down on the petal of a buttercup and called, "You can come out now!"

The Fairy peeked her head out of the bellflower and gasped, "How did you do that?"

"Easy." Emily raised her tiny pan flute. "With my magic flute."

"May I try it?" The Fairy reached for the flute.

"I'm the only one who can use it," Emily explained. "The great wizard Gallivant gave it to me at my coronation."

The Fairy stared at Emily. "You are a princess?"

Emily looked down at her clothes. She wasn't exactly dressed like a princess. She wore her short green riding skirt and leather-trimmed vest.

"I'm the Emerald Princess," she said in her most regal voice. "I rule the Greenwood."

"Isn't that funny?" The Fairy flew over to Emily's buttercup. "I'm a princess, too."

Emily's green eyes widened. "Really?"

"Well, I'm not a full princess yet. But

I'll be crowned one soon." The girl stuck out her hand. "I'm Arabell, from Fairy Land."

"Fairy Land?" Emily repeated. "I've heard of that place. But I've never ever seen it."

"That's because Fairy Land is hidden behind a large pink cloud," Arabell explained. "It's at the other end of the rainbow."

"The other end of the rainbow!" Emily repeated. "What an adventure it would be to go there!"

"Princess Emily!" a voice called from the distance. It was Arden the Unicorn. "I give up! I can't find you anywhere."

Emily leaped to her feet. "Oops. I forgot all about Arden. She doesn't know I'm down here."

Arabell fluttered her lavender wings

and rose into the air above the buttercup. "Is Arden a big white Unicorn with a beautiful pink-and-silver horn?"

"Yes," Emily called. "That's her. I'd answer her but she'd never hear me. I'm too small."

Arabell flew back to Emily's side. "Blow your flute and make yourself big again."

Emily made a face. "I can't do that, either. Once I make myself small, I have to stay that way until the sun sets."

"Princess Emily!" Arden's voice was getting farther and farther away.

Emily touched the Fairy's arm. "Would you fly to Arden and tell her I've shrunk?"

"I'm sorry, I can't!" Arabell cried. She zipped over to a tall stem of bellflowers and hid. "Someone might see me."

Emily grabbed a green vine and swung across to join Arabell on the bellflower. "What if they do?"

Arabell was still hiding. "They'll send word to the Fairy Queen in Fairy Land and I will be in very big trouble."

"Why?"

Arabell checked in all directions to make sure no creature — not a ladybug nor the smallest little flea — was listening. Then she said, "No one is allowed to leave Fairy Land without the queen's permission."

"The queen doesn't know you're gone?" Emily asked.

"No," Arabell whispered. "I ran away."

"Oh, Arabell!" Emily gasped. "That's terrible. Did something bad happen?"

Arabell nodded. "My mother had a baby."

Now Emily was confused. "The Fairy Queen had a baby?" she repeated. "Is it a bad baby?"

"Oh, no." Arabell's chin began to quiver. "He's a perfect baby. His name is Sweet William. And I love him. Everybody loves him."

"Then what is the matter?"

Arabell covered her face with her hands and burst into tears. "They all love Sweet William, and no one loves me!"

The Royal Bees

Arabell's tears were pale lavender. They dripped off her cheeks onto the bellflower's leaves.

"I'm sure your family loves you," Emily said, patting the Fairy's shoulder. She was extra careful not to touch Arabell's already bent wing. "I have three sisters and my parents love all of us."

"I have three sisters, too." Arabell

dabbed at the corner of her eye with a leaf. "But they don't care about me anymore. I can prove it."

"How?" Emily asked.

"Today is my birthday," Arabell said with a loud sniff. "And not one of them wished me happy birthday."

"Really?" Emily was surprised.

"My parents used to give me presents. But they didn't give me anything this year. Not even a card."

"That's terrible," Emily said with a frown.

Arabell's chin started to quiver again. "This morning I didn't go to breakfast or lunch, and no one noticed!"

Emily gave her new friend a hug. "That is the saddest story I've ever heard."

Another tear rolled down Arabell's cheek. "Now do you see why I ran away?"

Emily nodded. "If my parents forgot my birthday, I'd be very upset. But where are you going to go?"

Arabell shrugged. "I'm not sure. I didn't really plan this."

"I have an idea," Emily said. "You can come and live with me in the Emerald Palace!"

Arabell blinked her lavender eyes. "You have your own palace?"

"It's really more of a giant tree house."

"A tree house?" Arabell repeated.

"We can slide down ropes and sleep in hammocks. We can climb any tree we want, and swim in any pond." Emily clutched the Fairy Princess's hand. "Please say yes!"

Arabell's tears had dried. Her eyes had a new sparkle to them.

"It does sound fun," she whispered

excitedly. "But I can only stay for a little while. Long enough for my parents and family to miss me. But not so long that I miss my brother, Sweet William."

"It's a deal," Emily said.

She was about to say more, but a loud buzzing sound drowned out her words. "What's that awful noise?"

"Bees!" Arabell gasped. "The Royal Bees! They must be looking for me."

The Fairy Princess pointed through the tall stalks of lavender. Twenty yellow-and-black-striped bees were heading straight for them.

"They serve the Fairy Queen," Arabell whispered. "I have to hide."

She hopped behind the bellflower, leaving Princess Emily to talk to the Royal Bees.

The bee patrol flew in a V formation.

When they reached Emily, the head bee gestured with one leg for the others to wait. Then he flew to face Emily.

"Greetings," he said, loosening his green leather helmet. "We are looking for someone."

"Oh, who?" Emily waited for the bee to say Arabell, but his answer surprised her.

"We are looking for Nana Woodbine," the bee explained. "I'm told she lives somewhere in the land of the Greenwood."

Nana Woodbine was famous for her healing powers. Nana's mother had been half-Fairy and half-Woodsprite. Everyone in the Greenwood went to her when they were sick or hurt.

"Nana lives in a tiny cottage at the

Heart-o'-the-Wood," Emily replied. "Is someone ill?"

"Yes. Our Fairy Prince," the bee replied. "The Fairy Queen has asked us to find Nana Woodbine."

"The Fairy Prince!" Arabell quietly gasped from her hiding place. "But that's my brother!"

Princess Emily's eyes widened. "Excuse me, sir, but are you talking about Sweet William?"

The bee nodded. "He's been crying since lunch. They've tried everything. No one can get him to stop."

Emily pointed across the meadow. "If you fly straight through that stand of birch trees, you'll find a tiny cottage with bright red shutters. That's Nana's house."

"Thank you, miss." The bee spun in

midair and whistled to the other bees. In a flash they were gone.

Arabell came out from hiding. Her eyes were wide. Her skin was very pale.

"Sweet William never cries," Arabell said in a low voice. "Something must be terribly wrong. I have to go to him."

Emily nodded. "We'll get together another time."

Arabell put one hand to her cheek. "Wait! I can't go back to Fairy Land. At least not through the Rainbow Gate. Someone might see me! And the queen will know I ran away."

"But how did you get out of Fairy Land?" Emily asked.

"I followed a messenger out when the Rainbow Gate was open," Arabell said.

"Is the Rainbow Gate the only way to get into Fairy Land?" Emily asked.

"There is another way. Through the Back Gate. But no one ever uses it. It leads to the Under Down." The Fairy shivered. "That's a terrible place."

"Where is the Under Down?" Princess Emily asked.

"It's below a place called the Mysterious Forest," Arabell replied.

Now it was Emily's turn to shiver. The Mysterious Forest was a big dark shadow of trees that cut across the Jewel Kingdom. Princess Emily's parents had warned her never to go there. Bad things happened in that forest.

"Do you need a key to use the Back Gate?" Emily asked.

Arabell shook her head. "No. The roots and rats keep intruders away."

"I think you're going to have to go

through the Under Down if you want to see Sweet William," Emily said.

"I can't," Arabell moaned. "I'm too afraid."

"Don't say that," Emily cried. "You are a princess. Princesses never run from danger. We are the bravest of the brave."

The Fairy grabbed Emily's arm. "I'd be brave if you came with me."

Emily's eyes widened. "You mean, go under the earth with the roots and rats?"

"You said you wanted to go to the other end of the rainbow," Arabell reminded her. "You said it would be a great adventure."

"Did I say that?" Emily asked.

Arabell nodded. "Yes, you did."

Emily had wished for an adventure. And it looked like her wish had come true.

But she didn't know if she was ready for it. "I'd need to send a message to Arden first —"

"I'll fly you to her," Arabell cut in. "Please say you'll come."

Emily took a deep breath and held out her hand. "All right, Princess Arabell. Take me to Fairy Land."

To the Under Down

The entrance to the Under Down was a rotting stump at the edge of the Mysterious Forest. Sitting in front of it was a huge orange Wurm. It had no eyes, but it knew the princesses were there.

"Don't take another step," the Wurm said in a crackly voice. "I may be blind, but I can hear and smell you."

Arabell took one look at the slimy

orange Wurm and whimpered. "Oh, Emily, I don't think I can go into the Under Down."

Emily squeezed Arabell's arm. "Yes you can. Remember, you are a princess. Brave and strong."

"Tell me your names," the Wurm demanded.

Emily did the talking. She said, "This is Arabell, Princess of Fairy Land. She needs to get to the Back Gate."

"And who are you?" the Wurm asked, sniffing the air around Emily. "Are you a Fairy?"

"Why should that matter?" Emily asked.

"Because only Fairies are allowed to pass through our land. They are the only creatures we can trust in the Under Down," the Wurm explained. "And even Fairies must meet with Digger."

"Who's Digger?" Emily asked.

"He's a very fat, very ugly Moley-Poley," Arabell whispered into Emily's ear.

"Stop that whispering," the Wurm ordered. "Digger is our leader. And you'd better not call him fat or he'll throw you in the Pit."

The Pit sounded worse than rats and roots. Now Princess Emily was starting to feel a little weak in the knees.

"You still haven't answered my question," the Wurm said, slithering closer to Emily. "Are you a Fairy?"

Emily looked to Arabell for help. But Arabell didn't say a word.

"Of course I'm a Fairy!" Emily suddenly shouted. The princess backed into the meadow that edged the Mysterious Forest.

In the meadow grew a large cluster of

star lilies. Emily plucked two petals from the white-and-purple flower. She tucked them into the back of her skirt.

"Brilliant!" Arabell whispered to Emily.

Emily turned to the Wurm. "Here are my wings. You can feel them."

The Wurm sniffed Emily's flower petals. Emily held her breath.

Finally the Wurm said, "You may enter. But you'll have to ask Digger to open the Back Gate."

"And how do we find Digger?" Princess Emily asked as they followed a path of rotting leaves into the stump.

"Just step into that black hole," the Wurm said with a chuckle. "Don't worry about finding Digger. He'll find you."

5

The Moley-Poley

The princesses stepped into the black hole and slid down a dirt slide. They dropped onto something squishy. It felt like moss.

"Emily," Arabell said as they huddled together in the dark. "I'm scared. My heart is nearly jumping out of my chest."

Emily squeezed Arabell's hand so hard

it hurt. "I'm scared, too," she whispered. "But we can't show it."

Arabell nodded. "We're princesses —"

"Brave and bold," Emily finished with her.

They stared into the blackness. After a few minutes they saw hundreds of bright yellow circles all around them.

Arabell whispered into Emily's ear, "Did you see that? Two of those circles just blinked at me."

"I think those circles are eyes," Emily answered.

"Eyes?" Arabell choked.

"Be brave, Princess!" Emily reminded Arabell.

"I'm trying," Arabell said in a very shaky voice.

"Quit staring at us!" Emily shouted at

the top of her lungs. "It's very rude!"

"Leave us alone!" Arabell shouted just as loudly.

Suddenly the air was filled with loud squeaking. The yellow eyes blinked out.

"I guess we showed them," Emily said with a nervous laugh. "What do you think they were?"

"Rats or bats," Arabell answered. "Or toads or lizards. Or snakes or —"

"Stop!" Emily ordered. "I'm sorry I asked. Now, let's get going."

"I'm not sure where to go," Arabell whispered. "It's so dark, I can't see my hand in front of my face."

"Touch the wall," Emily said. "We'll follow it out of here. And maybe, if we're lucky, we won't have to meet any Moley-Poleys."

Emily put one fingertip against the wall. It was cold and slimy. Just touching it gave her goose bumps.

She and Arabell moved as quickly as they could through the black passage.

Every few feet they tripped over a tree root or caught their hair in a spiderweb. And every now and then something crawled across their hands. But the two princesses never screamed. They just kept moving.

"I'm coming, Sweet William," Arabell said to herself, over and over again.

"Me, too," Emily added.

After they'd walked for a very long time, they heard a noise.

Scritch. Scratch. Scritch.

"What was that?" Arabell whispered, turning her head toward the sound. "It sounds like scratching."

"Or digging," Emily said.

Scritch. Scratch. Scritch.

"There it is again." Arabell reached her hand into the blackness. "Ew! I touched something. It felt like a rat!"

Emily called into the dark. "Who's there? You'd better speak up if you know what's good for you."

Suddenly light filled the tunnel. A lit candle sat on a table in front of them.

Behind the table stood a big blob of an animal. His head was pale orange like the Wurm who guarded the stump. But his body was covered in shiny black fur. He had sharp pink claws. Behind him was the Back Gate.

"Digger?" Emily asked, trying not to be scared of the creature.

"That's my name, it ain't no shame."

As he spoke, the Moley-Poley dug at the dirt floor with his clawed feet.

"Let us pass," Emily said bravely. "We have to get to Fairy Land."

"Not so fast." Digger puffed himself up until his body blocked the entire Back Gate. "Digger only lets Fairies pass through this gate."

"But we *are* Fairies," Arabell replied.

Digger pointed to Emily. "If she's a Fairy, where are her wings?"

Arabell looked at Emily and gasped, "They're gone! Your wings must have fallen off in the tunnel."

The Moley-Poley squinted at Emily. "Fairies' wings don't fall off."

The Emerald Princess thought fast. "Of course my wings didn't fall off," she said. "Someone stole them. Someone with hundreds of yellow eyes."

Digger looked surprised. "The Slither stole your wings?" he asked.

Emily had never heard of a Slither but it sounded like a rotten creature.

"Yes, it did," she said boldly. "And that Slither tried to steal Arabell's, too. Show him, Princess."

Arabell panicked. "Show him what, Emily? What?"

"Your *wing*!" Emily said, very slowly. "The bent one. *Remember?*"

Arabell's eyes widened. "*Oh*, my bent wing."

She turned her back so Digger could see the wing Emily had dented in the Forest of Flowers. "See? There it is! And it still hurts!"

Digger looked at the bent lavender wing. Then he stared into Arabell's face to see if she was telling the truth.

Unfortunately Arabell looked like she was about to cry. The Emerald Princess couldn't let that happen.

"If you don't believe Arabell," Emily said, "why don't you give her a test? A Fairy test."

Digger's pink lips curled into a smile. "That I can do. A riddle-me-diddle. Fairies love riddle-me-diddles."

"Fine." Emily folded her hands across her chest. "Give Arabell a riddle-me-diddle."

"Oh, no." The Moley-Poley turned to Emily. "This riddle is not for Arabell. This riddle-me-diddle is for you."

Riddle-Me-Diddle

Emily liked riddles. But it had been a very long time since she'd solved one.

"Ready or not, here it comes," Digger cried. He left the Back Gate and rolled himself in front of Emily.

Emily saw the unguarded gate and said, "Before you start, don't you think Arabell should be out of the room? She might accidentally help me."

Digger snorted impatiently. "Arabell, stand by the Back Gate and don't cheat."

Once Arabell was at the Back Gate, Digger began.

"*All my life I eat. But when I drink I die. What am I?*"

Emily did not know the answer. But she pretended like she did.

"Ha! Ha! Ha!" she laughed. "That is one of my favorite riddles. Couldn't you have picked a harder one, Digger?"

Digger rolled closer to Emily. His wormy head was inches from her face.

"You don't know the answer," he whispered. "And you are no Fairy. I'm going to throw you into the Pit."

"The Pit!" Emily didn't even pause to think. She jabbed Digger in the belly. He instantly rolled into a ball. Then Emily shoved the Moley-Poley with all her might.

"Yeow!" Digger cried in surprise as he rolled backward across the floor.

"Run, Arabell!" Emily shouted. "Go through the Back Gate to Fairy Land."

"But what about you?" Arabell cried.

"Don't worry about me!" Emily called. "Just run!"

"Oh, no, you don't!" Digger growled as he tried to unroll himself.

The Emerald Princess moved quickly. She grabbed the candle with one hand and pushed Digger's table over with the other. Then she leaped through the Back Gate and out of the Under Down.

Holding the candle high, Emily followed Arabell up a flight of stone steps. At the top was a pool of sparkling water.

The air shimmered with rainbow-colored light.

"We made it," Arabell cried. "We're at the other end of the rainbow."

"Boy, am I glad to be here!" Emily said. "I don't think I could have pretended to be a brave princess for one more second."

Arabell giggled. "Me neither."

Emily dipped her candle in the water. There was a loud hiss as the flame went out.

"I've got it!" she cried.

"Got what?" Arabell asked.

"The answer to the riddle. All my life I eat. But when I drink, I die."

"What's the answer?" Arabell asked.

"Fire!" Emily held up the candle. "A flame needs air to burn. But water puts out the flame."

Arabell put her hands on her hips. "Well, well," she said, with a smile.

"Maybe you have a little bit of Fairy dust in you after all."

Emily wiggled her eyebrows. "Maybe I do."

Arabell pointed to the pink cloud floating high above the pool's waterfall. "There's Fairy Land. Take my hand and I'll fly you there."

"What are we waiting for?" Emily said. "Let's go help Sweet William."

Sweet William

———•◦•———

The Fairy Queen's castle was made of glass. Its six towers sparkled with tiny twinkly lights in the late afternoon glow.

"I've never seen anything so beautiful in my entire life," Princess Emily whispered as they entered the castle.

"The queen designed it herself,"

Arabell whispered back. "She's very proud of it."

The girls followed a golden staircase that wound its way into one of the towers. At the top of the stairs, they could hear a baby crying.

A man's voice carried over the baby's cries. "The prince must have eaten something that disagreed with him."

"That's Pennyroyal," Arabell whispered. "The oldest and wisest of our Fairy elders."

"But we've only fed him nectar and dewdrops," a lady's voice replied. "It couldn't be that."

Arabell squeezed Emily's arm. "That's my mother, the Fairy Queen."

"Why don't you tell her you're home?" Emily whispered. "It will probably make her feel better."

Arabell made a face. "I'm afraid."

"That she'll be angry with you for running away?" Emily asked.

Arabell nodded.

A different voice joined the queen's conversation. It was an older woman.

"Sweet William seems perfectly healthy. He doesn't have a fever and his skin feels cool and dry."

"I know that voice," Emily cried. "That's Nana Woodbine from the Greenwood. The Royal Bees must have flown her here. She's an excellent healer."

"I think something must have upset Sweet William," Nana said. "I'd like to try to give him some chamomile tea for his nerves."

"Chamomile?" Arabell gasped. "Sweet William can't stand chamomile."

As if in agreement, Sweet William cried even louder. "Waaaaah!"

"Perhaps a little peppermint," Pennyroyal added.

"Peppermint!" Arabell repeated. "That's even worse than chamomile."

"Go tell them!" Emily said, giving the princess a gentle shove forward.

"Tell the oldest and wisest Fairy in our land that he's wrong?" Arabell gasped. "I can't do that!"

Emily leaped forward. "After all we've been through? If you can't, I can!"

"Emily, wait!" Arabell whispered. "Something terrible could happen."

But Emily wasn't listening. She raced to the top of the stairs and into the nursery.

Arabell flew behind her. "Emily, please stop. You don't know my mother. She has a very bad temper."

Sweet William lay in a swan-shaped cradle. The Fairy Queen sat on a purple

velvet cushion next to him. She was beautiful. Her blonde hair was swept into a bun and an elegant crown circled her head. She had big lavender eyes like Arabell, and gauzy silver wings.

A bald-headed Fairy with bushy eyebrows and pointed ears bent over the cradle. "Here you go, little prince, drink up."

"No, stop!" Princess Emily shouted. "Get away from that baby!"

Pennyroyal leaped backward, spilling his tea. Two younger Fairies who were his assistants jumped back, too. Even Nana Woodbine, who had changed herself to Fairy size, stumbled back.

The Fairy Queen sprang to her feet. "Who are you? And what are you doing?"

"I'm here to help Sweet William,"

Emily replied. "Don't give him any tea. It will make him ill."

"Guards!" the Fairy Queen cried. "There is a stranger in the nursery. Seize her!"

The air was filled with a loud buzzing sound. The Royal Bees appeared from everywhere. They didn't look happy.

"Arabell!" Emily cried as the Royal Bees lifted her into the air. "Be brave. Help meeeeeee!"

Arabell suddenly flew out from behind the nursery door.

"Stop, Bees!" Arabell's voice boomed. "Put down that princess."

The Royal Bees hovered in midair, waiting for the queen's order.

"Arabell!" the queen cried. "Where have you been?"

"Never mind that, Mother," Arabell said in her bravest voice. "Tell the Royal Bees to put down my friend. That's Emily, the Emerald Princess."

The Fairy Queen gasped.

Emily, who was still hanging in the air, suddenly felt a tingling in her fingers and toes. That could only mean one thing. The magic flute's spell was about to wear off.

"Arabell!" Emily sang out. "Maybe we should go outside. The sun is setting."

"Huh?" Arabell didn't understand what Emily was talking about.

"When the sun sets," Emily explained, *"big things* happen."

"Big things?" Arabell's eyes widened. "Oh! *Big* things!"

The tiny princess turned to her mother, frantic. "Please, Mother. Tell the Royal Bees to take that princess outside."

The queen was confused. "But I thought you said — "

"Never mind!" Arabell cried as the big orange sun sank slowly behind the horizon. She raced to the nursery windows and threw them open. "Take her outside," she ordered the Bees.

Luckily for everyone, the Royal Bees obeyed. Because the second the sun slipped out of sight in Fairy Land, there was a loud bang.

And the Emerald Princess went from being Emily the Fairy to Emily the Giant.

Surprise!

When the Emerald Princess shot up to her normal size, it surprised everyone.

Princess Emily stood outside the tiny glass castle and peered through the window. Sweet William lay in his cradle, blinking up at her. He didn't make a sound. Neither did anyone else.

"The Fairy Prince has stopped crying!"

Pennyroyal finally whispered. "The Emerald Princess did it."

Nana Woodbine shook her head. "Princess Emily didn't stop Sweet William's tears. It was Arabell. Sweet William stopped crying the instant he heard her voice."

Arabell fluttered over to her brother's cradle. "Hello, Sweet William," she cooed.

"Bell?" the baby asked in a tiny voice.

"Bell is right here," Arabell said with a smile. "You don't need to cry anymore."

The baby giggled and clapped his tiny hands together. "Air-bell!"

Arabell tickled her brother under the chin with one finger. He squealed with delight.

"Why, look at that," Pennyroyal said to Nana Woodbine. "It's magic."

"That's not magic," Nana Woodbine replied. "That is love."

"It's clear, madam, that Sweet William doesn't need any doctors," Pennyroyal said to the queen. "He just needs his sister." He arched a bushy eyebrow at Arabell. "It was your running away that caused this whole problem."

"You know about that?" Arabell gasped.

"Well, of course he knows," the Fairy Queen replied. "We all know. We've been searching everywhere for the Birthday Princess."

"Birthday Princess?" Arabell repeated.

The Fairy Queen touched the tip of Arabell's nose. "That's you, my dear."

Arabell's eyes filled with lavender tears.

"Did you hear that, Emily?" she called to the Emerald Princess. "My family didn't forget my birthday."

"How could we forget?" the Fairy Queen said. "All we've done for the last four days is plan your party."

The Fairy Queen took her daughter's hand and flew onto the balcony, where Emily was waiting.

The queen pointed to the castle garden. Hundreds of Fairies had gathered by the pond.

"The party was supposed to be a surprise," the queen explained, "but you disappeared."

"I'm just lucky I met Princess Emily," Arabell said, smiling up at the Emerald Princess. "I was lost and scared, but Emily helped me get home."

"Thank you, Emily," the queen said with a royal nod.

"I didn't really do much, Your Majesty," Emily said, blushing.

"You did, too!" Arabell said. "You led us through the Under Down. You faced a huge orange Wurm, a Slither with a thousand eyes, and that awful Moley-Poley."

The Fairy Queen blinked in surprise. "My, my! You two have had a very big adventure!"

Emily curtsied to the queen. "Yes, we have. Bigger than I ever imagined."

"But Emily remained brave to the very end," Arabell added.

"I'm not surprised," the queen chuckled. "Emily, you are your mother's daughter."

Now it was Emily's turn to be surprised. "You know my mother?"

The queen smiled mysteriously. "Almost as well as I know myself."

Before the Fairy Queen could explain, trumpets sounded from the garden below. A purple-and-white birthday cake floated to the center of the pond.

"Could Emily have cake with us and stay for my birthday party?" Arabell asked the Fairy Queen.

"Princess Emily may stay as long as she likes," the Fairy Queen replied. "We're going to have dancing, magic tricks, and dragonfly rides. And at midnight, you will get to make your birthday wish."

It all sounded wonderful to the Emerald Princess. But now that Emily was her normal size, she felt out of place.

"I would love to stay for your party," Princess Emily said. "But I'm too big to stay in Fairy Land."

"Mother? Do I have to wait until

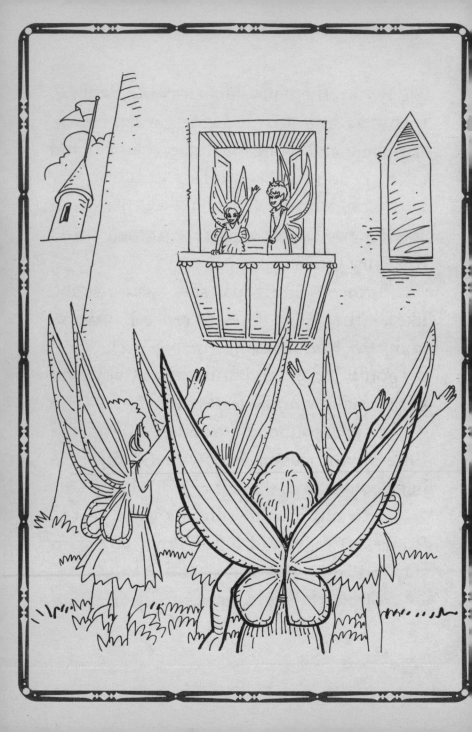

midnight to make my wish?" Arabell asked.

The queen thought for a second. "No, I don't suppose you do. You could make your wish right now, if you like."

Arabell grinned. "Here's my wish. That Emily, the ruler of the Greenwood and Emerald Princess of the Jewel Kingdom, could be just my size for the rest of the night."

The Fairy Queen looked at Emily. "Would you like that?"

"I'd love it," Emily whispered.

"Then it's done."

With a wave of her wand, the queen said to Emily, "Your wish is granted."

Emily instantly shrank back to Fairy size.

Arabell clapped her hands in delight.

"Now you can stay for the whole party. And the whole night!"

The two friends hugged each other, and Emily cried with glee, "Now *that* will be a fun adventure!"

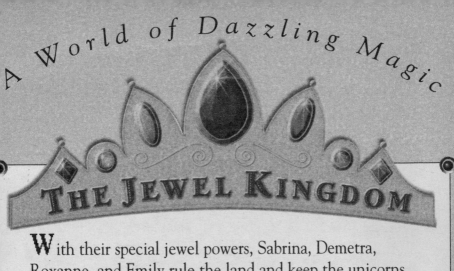

A World of Dazzling Magic

THE JEWEL KINGDOM

With their special jewel powers, Sabrina, Demetra, Roxanne, and Emily rule the land and keep the unicorns, dragons, nymphs, and other wonderful creatures safe. Join them for adventure after adventure full of dazzling magic!

- ❏ BCF-21283-4 **#1 RUBY PRINCESS RUNS AWAY** \$3.99
- ❏ BCF-21284-2 **#2 THE SAPPHIRE PRINCESS MEETS A MONSTER** \$3.99
- ❏ BCF-21287-7 **#3 THE EMERALD PRINCESS PLAYS A TRICK** \$3.99
- ❏ BCF-21289-3 **#4 THE DIAMOND PRINCESS SAVES THE DAY** \$3.99
- ❏ BCF-11713-0 **#5 THE RUBY PRINCESS SEES A GHOST** \$3.99
- ❏ BCF-11714-9 **#6 THE SAPPHIRE PRINCESS HUNTS FOR TREASURE** \$3.99
- ❏ BCF-11738-6 **#7 THE EMERALD PRINCESS FINDS A FAIRY** \$3.99

Available wherever you buy books, or use this order form.

Scholastic Inc., P.O. Box 7502,
2931 East McCarty Street, Jefferson City, MO 65102

Please send me the books I have checked above. I am enclosing $_____
(please add $2.00 to cover shipping and handling).
Send check or money order — no cash or C.O.D.s please.

Books #1-#4 come with beautiful, glittering jewel necklaces — collect them all!

Name_____Age _____

Address_____

City _____State/Zip _____

Please allow four to six weeks for delivery. Offer good in the U.S. only. Sorry, mail orders are not available to residents of Canada. Prices subject to change.

JK997